The Depot

Book 2 in Haunted Depot: The Ghost Curse

Kristy K. James

(originally as J.J. Belding)

I would like to dedicate this book to Kathie who, once again, has spent countless hours helping me to make another story the best it can be.

Dear Friend,

Consider this your welcome to Hemisphere. You might think your presence here is an accident. Maybe you believe you just stumbled onto our website, liked what you saw, and decided to check us out. Or that you simply found yourself here while on a leisurely drive.

Well, you'd be wrong.

It was fate.

Yes, you're here because fate led you here. Because *you* are meant to be here. Why? That remains to be seen. Maybe you'll wind up calling Hemisphere your home. Maybe we're just a stop in the road on your way to somewhere else. Maybe you'll remember your time with us. Most do not.

One thing is for sure though, you'll never find another place like Hemisphere. It's one-of-a-kind.

Hemisphere is a unique location, steeped in mysticism. *All* are welcome within our boundaries. We'd like to tell you there's a simple explanation for the things you may see or experience during your stay. A little theatrical drama, if you will. But it wouldn't be true. Here in Hemisphere, the things that go bump in the night are very real.

If you decide to stay past sundown, we encourage you to read the Visitors Orientation Packet. The warning about "calamity or death by misadventure?" It's not a joke.

It would behoove you to follow the advice inside. We also suggest traveling in groups, or hiring a local "guide" to show you around our beautiful town.

Common sense should tell you to use caution when hiking in any unfamiliar area. The forests and cliffs surrounding Hemisphere are beautiful. They are also home to a variety of wild creatures found nowhere else on earth. Don't be caught unaware. It should go without saying – stay out of the woods and off the cliffs after dark.

Again, welcome to Hemisphere. Fate has led you to our area. What happens next is up to you. Choose wisely.

Get the insider's guide to navigating Hemisphere FREE when you sign up for our newsletter!

From safety tips, to the Hemisphere Business Directory, to our late night Food Delivery Guide, to a map so you can find your way around town, the Orientation and New Residents Packet has it all. Simply click on the link below. Subscribers will also be the first to know about new releases and special offers. And you can rest assured knowing your information will stay safely with us (no selling or sharing) – and we'll never spam you.

http://www.subscribepage.com/d8n7d2

Chapter 1

The first thing that went through Kate Proctor's sleep-fogged mind was that this was the first time she'd woken up in this room and didn't smell coffee. Or bacon. Or something that meant someone she loved was up and around and stirring about in the kitchen. Stirring about and waiting for her to come down.

No one would ever be waiting for her again. Not here.

The second thing that went through her mind was that she'd signed a two year contract for the phone that was currently beeping loudly on the night stand. A contract that was costing her more than fifty dollars a month – just for the phone. And she would continue to be billed for it for the next year and a half – whether she threw it against the wall or not.

Sighing, she grabbed it anyway but instead of smashing it to a million bits, she slid the option that would allow her to snooze for another five minutes. And then she closed her eyes, willing herself to doze back off.

She wasn't ready to get up yet. She didn't want to deal with the responsibilities that awaited her once she was dressed and ready for the day.

Except she never dozed back off. She always set the alarm to go off precisely when she wanted to get up. Except today. She didn't want to start going through her grandparent's things. She didn't want to pay a visit to the police station. And she didn't want to start making decisions she couldn't undo. Like visiting the depot and trying to figure out whether she was finally ready to sell it or not.

She was ninety-nine percent certain she *would* sell it. But it was that teeny, tiny little one percent that had kept her tossing and turning most of the night. It was her grandfather's favorite place in the whole world and there were so many special memories she associated with it. Memories marred by the fact that he was murdered there but still, most were good.

Another sigh and she was flinging back the quilt Grandma Clara had made for her fifteenth birthday. Back then, Kate hadn't appreciated the patience, love, and time that had gone in to creating such a beautiful masterpiece. She did now though and as she pushed herself to a sitting position, she ran a finger over the even rows of perfect stitches.

She'd have to take it home with her this time. Because if she did what she'd come here to do, she wouldn't be returning to Hemisphere again. The thought made her heart ache and so she shoved it to a hidden corner of her mind. It would have to stay there until she was ready to deal with it.

"You've only got two weeks so you'd better be ready soon," she reminded herself, swinging her legs over the edge of the mattress and sliding her feet into the warm, fuzzy bunny slippers waiting for her. It shouldn't have surprised her to find them sitting on the foot of her bed, washed and closed safely in a clear plastic shoe box. Grandpa would have been the last one to handle them after she'd gone home last Thanksgiving.

She swallowed the lump that formed in her throat, blinked back tears that filled her eyes, and padded off to the bathroom down the hall.

Someone had thoughtfully covered all of the furniture with sheets and tarps following Merle Proctor's funeral. She hadn't thought about it at the time and was grateful someone else had. Now she only had to deal with the sinks and countertops, both in the bathroom and the kitchen. They were covered with more than nine months' worth of dust.

She added a thorough cleaning to a rapidly growing mental list. It was getting long enough, she knew she'd have to make a list on her phone. There wasn't enough time to risk forgetting anything.

After she dressed, Kate made a pot of coffee, pouring a cup to drink at the house, then filling a thermos to carry with her in the car as she set about trying to deal with things she couldn't ignore anymore.

First on today's agenda was a trip to the Hemisphere Police Department. But the thought of demanding answers as to why Merle's killer hadn't been found yet quickly moved that chore down a spot on her to-do list. Maybe she'd swing by Big Ed's. She hadn't been there since she'd come back for the funeral. This might be her last chance to have one of the best breakfasts she'd ever eat.

"HEY, SWEETHEART," GLORIA, a slender woman with short, graying hair said softly, wrapping strong arms around her in a tight hug. "We weren't sure we'd ever see you around here after the funeral."

"I wasn't sure you would either," Kate whispered, blinking back tears that filled her eyes again.

Even as she said the words though, she knew they were a lie. No matter how much it hurt to come back, she'd always known she would. That she had to. As the sole beneficiary, she had an obligation to deal with her grandparents estate, ordinary as it was. Besides, there were some special things she'd never entrust to the care of strangers.

"You want the usual?" Gloria asked, clearing her throat, then linking arms with Kate and leading her to *her* stool at the counter.

"What else would I get?" she asked, hoping she managed to sound at least a little cheerful even though it was hard to talk past the lump in her throat. As she sat down, Big Ed looked up, smiled sadly, and winked at her.

"She's having the usual," Gloria told him, pouring Kate a cup of coffee.

"I know. I started it as soon as I saw her walk through the door."

He smiled again and lifted a partially cooked piece of french toast. There would be two more on the grill too, along with three slices of bacon. When it was finished, he'd top the toast with fresh, real butter, and a thick sprinkling of powdered sugar.

Her grandpa had introduced her to the delicious combination when she'd been a girl and she'd fallen in love with it after the first bite. Try as she might though, she'd never been able to replicate the exact taste, not in the kitchen at her apartment and certainly not at the restaurant she managed.

"Mind if I join you?" Ed asked, nodding at an empty stool beside her. "Things have slowed down and I could do with a break."

"Be my guest," Kate said, glad for the company. He'd always been one of her favorite people though when he set his soft brown eyes on her, like he was doing now, she'd have sworn he could see things no one else had ever seen.

"Are you holding up okay?" he finally asked when she was about half finished with the food. It wasn't unusual for him to just sit quietly with the object of his attention. It also wasn't uncommon for him to talk their ear off. Usually, he managed to hit a happy medium.

Today, she wished he'd just stayed quiet because she wasn't sure how to answer him. If he were anyone else, she'd have just told him what he wanted to hear. That she was okay. That she'd moved on and remembered Merle and Cora with fondness but life was fine. Except it wasn't and she knew if she tried to get away with telling him that, he'd just level her with *the* look and ask again. So she told him the truth.

"I miss him," she whispered, not meeting his eyes. "I miss them both."

"So do I, Katie, so do I" he said sadly, laying an open hand, palm up on the counter.

When she laid hers on top, his dark fingers closed around hers and she was struck by how pale her skin was. Of course, she hadn't been outside much this year. All she'd done was work and go home so she hadn't been exposed too much sun.

"Why would anyone want to hurt him?" she asked, resting her head against his shoulder. "He never harmed anyone in his life."

"I know. I've asked myself the same question a thousand times. Your grandfather was one of the kindest, gentlest souls I've ever known. And if I find his killer before the police do..."

He didn't finish the thought but Kate knew what he'd been going to say. She'd probably said the same thing, or something very much like it, many times herself. Each time she'd phoned the police to see if there were any new leads and each person she asked always said no.

"I WISH I COULD TELL you that we had more, Ms. Proctor," Sergeant Daniel Corgan was saying as he walked her to the main door. "But there were no witnesses, no fingerprints, no murder weapon. Not even a foot or tire print to give us a clue."

"Maybe you missed something?"

Even as she asked the question, she knew it was a waste of time. The officer seemed very competent. She didn't think he'd have overlooked anything. It was just so hard to accept that whoever had killed her grandfather was going to get away with it. That someone could take the life of that sweet, generous man and walk away without so much as a slap on the wrist, much less the life in prison – or death penalty – he deserved was wrong. So very wrong.

"I'm sorry. I wish I had better news. Believe me, no one would like to solve this case more than me." He sounded sincere. When Kate glanced at him, she could see he was almost as frustrated as she was. "I haven't been here long but I did meet your grandfather a few times. He was a nice man. He didn't deserve this."

"Thank you. I appreciate you saying it."

"I'm not just saying it."

"I know. I – uh – guess I should get going. I wanted to stop by the depot. Have a look around. And then I should pick up a few groceries."

Eating in the local restaurants brought back wonderful memories but it wouldn't take long for her to start putting on extra pounds if she didn't start preparing her own meals. Of course, if she wanted to be honest with herself, she'd admit that the more time she spent with people she'd come to care about through the years, the harder it would be to say goodbye forever.

"You ... visited here often when you were a kid?" For the first time, Daniel Corgan seemed a bit uncomfortable.

"Yes. Every summer and most holidays. Why?"

"You know it's ... a good idea to be in before dark?"

"Yes. I know."

"All right then. If I can be of further assistance, you know where I am."

With that, he held the door open and Kate headed out into the chilly gray drizzle that had been falling since the night before.

Hemisphere was a strange town, she thought, unlocking the door of her silver Mazda. She'd never seen anything happen, or heard anything specific that *might* happen, but her grandparents had been adamant about staying safely locked in the house between the hours of dusk and dawn. And since they'd seemed genuinely concerned, she'd always made a point to do so. Just in case, it was a habit she didn't intend to start breaking now.

Not quite ready to face the next item on her list, Kate made a right on Oak Street and headed for Stoller's Point. In under two minutes, she'd pulled to a stop alongside the overlook, grabbed her umbrella from the backseat, and was standing next to the balustrade beside the cliffs and water in Stoller's Channel and Sleeping Bear Harbor.

Her grandparents had brought her here often. It had been one of her favorite places. Today, it just brought to mind more bittersweet memories. She didn't have any bread to feed the gulls that screeched and circled overhead. When they figured out they were wasting their time with her, they headed back out to the beach, searching the whitecaps for their lunch.

The lightweight fall jacket she'd grabbed on the way out of the house wasn't heavy enough to protect her from the bitter wind blowing across the water. She wouldn't be able to stay long but since she'd likely never set eyes on this place again, she wanted to see it one last time.

Just the thought of never coming back was breaking her heart but there was nothing here for her anymore. Sure, there were a handful of acquaintances who could turn into friendships if she had more time but they weren't enough to keep drawing her back. Not like Grandma and Grandpa had been. Without them here, what was the point?

With more determination than she'd felt since crawling out of bed a few hours ago, Kate headed back to the car. It was time.

HER GRANDPA HAD ONLY ever referred to it as 'The Depot' but it was so much more than that. Sure, the huge main building was still there, still covered in half a century's worth of dust. Spooky cobwebs still hung from the corners and rafters, casting eerie shadows against the wall when the sun hit the skylight just right.

An ancient thirteen room hotel sat just to its southwest, along with three broken down sheds that were scattered around the grounds. A ramshackle overhang housing an eighty year old, broken down steam engine, box car, and passenger car sat beside the long unused tracks.

So technically, it was a bit more than a depot, covering a full city block. It was located at the southernmost edge of town, near the intersection of Old Stoney Point Road and County Road 13.

There were mature trees here and there, along with knee high weeds, cracked and broken pavement. And sometimes frightening shadows.

Today, a man in a suit was also there, standing several yards away from a bright red sports car. Kate parked on the other side of the lot and pulled a can of pepper spray and a small jackknife from her purse before getting out. She pocketed the knife but kept the spray in her right hand and her cell phone in her left.

"You're trespassing," she called out, holding the can out when he made to approach her. "Don't come any closer."

"Oh, hey!" he said, coming to an abrupt halt and holding his hands out in a gesture of peace. "I'm sorry. I've been coming here for years. Merle Proctor, the last owner, knew and was okay with it. He knew I was a lover of history."

"Well, I'm the new owner and I'm not comfortable with you being here." She knew she sounded rude but between being nervous about his presence and the fact that this was her and her grandfather's special place, she wanted him gone.

"Kate Proctor?" he asked, taking a step backward when she raised the can at face level. "Wait! You have to remember me. Brad Jones? You know, 'Jones'ing for a new home? Give me a call at Jones Realty?' I've been sending you letters for the past few months because I have a client who's interested in buying the property. *That* Brad Jones?"

The top of the Brad Jones Realty stationary had both the cheesy jingle and a head shot of his perfectly chiseled, handsome face. Still, she just wanted to be left alone. She wanted to remember when life was better. When there were two people who truly loved and wanted her. Two people who were gone now, leaving her pretty much alone in the world.

"Look, Mr. Jones. I'm sorry. I've got a lot on my mind right now. I haven't even decided whether I want to sell or not. So please, just leave. I'd really like some time to think."

"I understand. If you do decided to sell though, the buyer is ready to sign the contract without delay," he said after an uncomfortable silence. For a moment, she thought he might have something to add but all he did was smile, offer a quick wave, then he climbed into his car and drove away. She didn't relax her stance until he was well out of sight.

She started to wonder how he knew she was here but then shook her head. It was Hemisphere. Her grandparents had lived here all their lives and school vacations and summers, she'd spent a third of her life here as well. Anyone she'd seen this morning could have mentioned she was in town.

Wandering around the grounds, she kept her hand wrapped firmly around the pepper spray. Maybe it was the overcast day, or that the nearest building with people in it was a block and a half down the road, but she was just the tiniest bit creeped out. Still, there was the feeling that she'd come home and she spent a little time peering in windows that had long since had the glass broken out by vandals.

The stories Grandpa had spun as they'd sat inside on sunny days, sipping sodas and munching on candy bars brought a sad smile to her face. He'd made the depot seem exciting, talking about the old days when it had been bustling with activity. Trains chugging through town twice a day. Passengers getting off because they'd reached their destination, or just to have a soda or ice cream at the counter in the far corner.

He'd paint a word picture so vivid, she could see it all unfolding around her. The dirt, the shadows, the gloom, all of it disappeared as men, women, and children – all dressed in colorful period clothing milled about the pristine white tile floor. She could almost smell the popcorn a vendor in the corner sold in red and white bags and hear the clink of spoons against the glass sundae dishes.

But Grandpa wasn't here anymore and the visions she'd been enjoying disappeared as abruptly as they'd come. Wiping away a tear that was sliding down her cheek, Kate turned and headed back to her car.

She had one more stop to make before heading back to the house. She'd come back here tomorrow. It was supposed to be clear and sunny. Maybe then, she'd be able to figure out what she wanted to do with everything. In the back of her mind though, she knew there was only one thing *to* do. She just didn't want to actually *make* that decision.

THE GRASS WAS WET FROM the drizzle so Kate just knelt beside the double width headstone. She traced the letters of their names with one finger. Merle Thomas Proctor and Clara Marie Proctor.

"I miss you both so much," she whispered, afraid if she spoke out loud, she might start to cry. "I don't have anyone anymore. After Mom and Dad found out you left everything to me, well, they won't even call to ask for money anymore. Not that I'd been giving them any for the past few years."

No, her co-workers finally made her see that she was just enabling them and she had just stopped one day. Still, they came around near holidays and their birthdays in hopes she'd change her mind. She never did but they never gave up hope that she would.

"Dad was so sure you'd give it all to them. I mean, it's not like it's a big loss or anything but at least I could say I had some sort of family left. Now I don't even have them. When he found out all you left him was that box of books... He was furious. Said he didn't want any 'stupid old books' and if I didn't give them half of the inheritance, I was dead to them."

They'd never been big on the whole parenting thing. Sometimes though, they'd pretend. When they wanted something. Money, usually, so they could buy more pot or beer. That's all they really cared about. That and partying.

Never her though. She hadn't heard from them since that day. Sometimes, it hurt so bad she wanted to cry. Other times, she had to smile. Within the pages of the books, her grandparents had hidden ten-thousand dollars.

"I don't know what to do, Grandpa. I've made a life for myself. I've got a good job, a nice apartment." An apartment that never really felt like home, a quiet part of her brain whispered. "What am I supposed to do? Give it all up and move to this weird little town? A place where you both acted like there were things that went bump in the night?"

Not that she was really afraid during her visits. It had all just been crazy stories, hadn't it? It was just the town taking the Fortnight of Fright Festival, something meant to be fun and a little creepy, a little too far.

"I know we all talked about me moving here. And I really did think about it sometimes. But now- You're both gone. At least I have friends at work." *Friends* she didn't socialize with outside of the restaurant. "I just don't know."

She knelt there, staring at the words engraved on the shiny gray slate, until she realized her hair and jacket were wet. Until the wind picked up and she shivered.

It was time to pick up a few groceries and get back to the house. Maybe she'd take tonight to just binge watch some of the comedies Grandpa collected. Make a quick supper, then snack the rest of the night. Until she was too tired to do anything but fall asleep. Until she was too tired to dream.

As she walked back to the car, she didn't even bother trying to wipe away the tears that fell from her eyes. The only stability she'd ever had in her life had been stolen from her. One from cancer, one from a killer who seemed to have gotten away with his crime. Or her crime.

If only there was some way to find out who did it. Maybe then, she could make a decision without the pain and guilt that had been eating away at her since the funeral, when she first realized she'd have to deal with a situation she wished hadn't been dumped in her lap. But after more than nine months, she'd still done nothing. She needed to figure out what she was going to do.

AFTER ANOTHER NIGHT spent tossing and turning, Kate woke up the next morning, grabbed her grandfather's handgun from the lock box he'd always kept hidden in his bedroom closet, then got an early start. The sun was barely over the horizon when she headed for the depot

Five minutes later, gun tucked in the waistband of her jeans, hidden by cardigan sweater, Kate unlocked the door to the hotel. It struck her as ridiculous that it was still locked when most of the windows had been broken out.

As she wandered from room to room, ducking under one massive cobweb after another, her heart hurt. Not only were windows gone but vandals had also spray painted graffiti on most of the walls. Some were declarations of love, some were weird pictures. The rest seemed to be a contest in who could come up with the foulest language on the planet, a few even in Spanish, if she remembered what she'd learned in the required eleventh grade class. Not that the teacher taught *those* words.

Worn and broken furniture from eras long past reminded her of elderly people walking slowly, hunched over as time bent their spines forward. All in all, it was a depressing sight and she described what she saw in a note-taking program on her phone.

"It doesn't look much different from when I was a kid," she said softly, her gaze scanning each room she walked through. "I guess I'm just seeing it with different eyes now. I never realized how sad it was back then."

After she'd made the rounds, she dutifully locked the door and turned her attention toward the depot. But she couldn't bear the thought of going through it just yet so she headed for a tree in the northeast corner.

It was the prettiest spot on the property. It always had been with the only grassy spot left. Everything else was just concrete that should have been torn up years ago or hard packed dirt. One of her favorite places, she sat down and leaned back against the tree. Her drifting thoughts landed on Hannah and Kate felt another twinge of pain in her already battered heart.

For nearly three years, she'd considered Hannah to be her best friend. They'd hung out every day from the time she was twelve until just after her fifteenth birthday. When the girl and her family moved away, Kate had cried for days. She almost cried now, remembering how much she missed her then. She still missed her, nearly as much, today.

"Enough," she muttered, jumping to her feet and dusting her jeans off. "You're not here to reminisce."

Nope. She was here to make a decision. To figure out what to do so she could get on with her life and not have it hanging over her head forever.

Again, she unlocked a door that was as useless as tits on a boar hog. She laughed when the saying came to mind. It had been one of her grandpa's favorites and he'd used it often. It was very applicable to this situation.

Thankful for the bright sunlight on the chilly autumn day, Kate wandered from one end of the large room to the other. Except for the cubicle where tickets were sold, two tiny restrooms, and the corner ice cream fountain, all that remained in the depot were broken, splintered benches and a few decades worth of dust and cobwebs.

She didn't bother to turn on the recorder this time because if she ever lost the phone and anyone heard her talking to Merle, they'd have thought she'd lost her mind.

"Those were the best days of my life, Grandpa. I wish you were still here. I wish you could tell me what to do. I feel like such a traitor even thinking about selling the place but it'll just keep sitting empty when I go back home. There doesn't seem to be much point in keeping it."

"What if you had a really good reason to keep it?" a soft, deep voice asked from behind her.

Chapter 2

She'd definitely grown up, he thought watching her whirl around, the handgun aimed directly at his heart. Like Brad Jones had done yesterday, he held his hands up in front of him in a gesture of surrender – even though she couldn't hurt him no matter how hard she tried.

"Who are you?" she demanded, her voice shaking nearly as much as the hands that held the gun.

"Ezra Hutchinson, ma'am."

"Why are you here? What do you want?" She bit the corner of her lower lip, something she'd always done when she was nervous or scared. It was a habit she'd had since she was a kid.

"That's easy. I'm hoping I can convince you to not sell this place."

"Why?"

"Now that's harder to explain. Your grandfather can do that better than I can."

"Grandpa's dead."

"I know, and I'm more sorry than I can say about that. He always meant to tell you about the depot but he told me he just never found the right moment." Ezra paused, trying to gauge how receptive she might be to what he wanted to tell her. He was guessing, on a scale of one to ten, that'd be about a zero. Okay. Plan B. His Plan B, not Merle's. "Your grandpa has a stack of journals back at the house. Diaries, if you will."

"How would you know something like that?" Her tone hadn't softened even a little but he could tell this was information she hadn't been aware of.

"I've known your grandfather for years. We were great friends. He used to bring them here to write and draw. He keeps them in a safe at the house."

"There is no safe at the house."

"Yes, there is. It's in the small pantry in the kitchen. If you pull out the lower shelf and push against the wall, it will unlock it. The combination should be in the will. I hope you'll take some time to read them, Kate. If you do, you'll see how important it is to keep this place in your family."

"Why would my grandpa keep journals and not tell me about it?"

"Maybe because he didn't want you to know about them? Maybe because he wanted you to have them after he was gone? I don't know. That's something you'd have to ask him."

"Well I can't now, can I?"

"You're a lot angrier than I remember you," he murmured, wondering if the sweet girl was still hiding somewhere beneath the tough exterior. He hoped so because if she wasn't, they didn't stand a chance of convincing her to stay.

"You remember me?" she scoffed, laughing. "I don't ever remember seeing you so I don't know how you can say such a thing."

"Please? Just go home and read the journals. It will explain so much better than I can. And when you're finished, come back and we can talk about your options. Please?" He took a slow step toward her and almost chuckled when her hands steadied and she held the gun out a little more. "Don't worry, I'm leaving. I'll keep well away from you, though you've never had anything to fear from me." As he reached toward the door handle, he turned and said softly, "You've grown into a lovely young woman, Kate. It was good to see you again. Oh. Start reading around mid-1967."

HE KNEW HER? THE THOUGHT kept running through her mind as she drove home. Unlike the man yesterday, this one hadn't made her as nervous. She hadn't been entirely comfortable though but- There was something vaguely familiar about him. Nothing she could really bring to the front of her mind, just a knowledge from somewhere that he wouldn't hurt her.

Right now, that wasn't important. All she really cared about was seeing if his story about the safe and the journals was true.

Grandpa kept a diary? More than one if Mr. Hutchinson was to be believed. The thought was astounding because tenderhearted as Merle Proctor had been, she just couldn't wrap her mind around that thought. Yes, he'd been very talented at pencil drawings but writing? Of course, there was a world of difference between writing stories and writing thoughts out so she supposed it wasn't out of the realm of possibility.

As soon as she got back to the house, she went directly to the pantry, dropped to her knees, and held her breath as she tugged gently on the bottom shelf. It slid out easily and her heart seemed to skip a beat. Wasting no time, Kate quickly moved a dozen or so dusty cans to the shelf above before pulling it the rest of the way out.

Then, holding her breath, she pushed against the wall. Nothing happened. The air whooshed out of her lungs as disappointment settled over her. He'd lied. The man named Ezra had lied. She hadn't realized how much she'd been counting on finding those journals, a tie to the man who had been the only real father figure in her life. But there were no journals. No safe. No secret hiding spot in the house.

Push harder.

Kate almost jumped when the thought popped into her head. It sounded so real, so close, she glanced behind her to see if anyone was there.

When her breathing slowed to normal again, she pushed against the panel a little harder and heard a soft click. Part of the wall popped away from the rest and she eased it open with her fingers, tensing because she half expected something to jump out.

To her surprise, a good size safe *was* sitting there. Gingerly, she reached in and tried to tug it forward. It was heavier than she expected so she pulled a little harder but it didn't budge so much as an inch, not even when she tried rocking it from side-to-side. So she just sat there staring at it at it for several long moments, marveling at the fact that her grandfather had kept something like this hidden, likely for many, many years. She wondered if her grandmother had known about it.

When the novelty wore off, she ran up to her bedroom to get the will from a pocket in her suitcase.

Surprisingly, she found the combination, just as Ezra Hutchinson said. It was near the end of the third page but it was there.

Holding her breath, she turned the dial, making sure she hit the exact numbers in each direction. Soon, she pulled the door open and gasped in surprise.

Not only was there a stack of leather bound journals, but several thick bundles of hundred dollar bills had been hidden behind them. It looked like a small fortune. Of course, her grandparents hadn't really trusted banks so it shouldn't have been a surprise to find they'd saved a lot of their money at the house.

Hands shaking, Kate pulled five journals out of the safe and set them on the table. She then pulled out the stacks of cash and felt a little sick to her stomach. There were nine three or four inch thick stacks of hundred dollar bills. It *was* a small fortune.

As tempted as she was to count it, Kate left it alone because she was more anxious to see what was in the journals. More curious to know what her grandfather had spent so much time writing about.

She carried them to the living room where she set them on the coffee table, then returned to the kitchen to make a cup of green tea. Since she intended to settle in and read for a while, she'd need at least a little caffeine.

She hadn't counted on getting sucked into a story so crazy and out of this world it could rival any work of fiction. With each turn of a page, she had to keep reminding herself that her grandfather – *her grandfather* – the only stable male influence in her life had written it.

June 19, 1967

I'd like to say it feels as though I've walked out of Hemisphere and onto the set of The Twilight Zone except I've always suspected that show was based on this town. If it wasn't, well, it should have been. Because what happened today- I still can't believe it, or the fact that I didn't run away crying and screaming like a little girl. On the off chance it was all a dream, I'm not going to say what happened. Or what might have happened. Not until I go back tomorrow.

I can't believe I'm even contemplating going back to the depot again. I've never been so scared I almost wet myself. That's how scared I was this afternoon though. But I have to know. I have to know if it's real or just a dream influenced by a dreary day, ominous shadows, and an overactive imagination.

Kate felt her stomach drop as she read the words. Something frightened Merle Proctor – the bravest man she'd ever known – so much that he was afraid to even write it down? So much he'd not gone back the next day at all. Or for the following two.

June 23, 1967

Ezra Hutchinson is real. Or as real as a man can be after being murdered ninety-five years ago. I still can't believe I'm writing this. Or that I'm admitting to myself that I spent the afternoon talking to a dead man. But I did. Part of me wants to laugh at the impossibility of it all. Another part wants me to check myself in at the Hemisphere Memorial, destination: psych ward.

But I'm not crazy. He was there. And he's real. And I'm going to take my journal tomorrow so I can draw him. I think I could do it now because after staring at him for three solid hours, probably with my mouth hanging open like an idiot, I've memorized every line and angle of his face. But I want to get him exactly right. He deserves that. I can't believe I'm saying that about a former train robber. He's had nearly a century to reform though, and I believe he has.

What's so astounding about the whole thing though is that Ezra is real. I mean real as in we shook hands. We shared some of my mother's oatmeal cookies. We talked about everything from the weather, to present day politics, to cute girls.

Trembling, Kate could hardly bring herself to turn the page. Grandpa had been quite the artist, at least when it came to pencil drawings. She had two notebooks full of pictures he'd drawn of her and Grandma through the years. They were amazingly good and she knew the one she was going to be seeing in a moment would be of the man she'd seen at the depot today. Ezra Hutchinson.

But she couldn't make herself do it. She wasn't ready for this. Two entries into his journal and she already needed a break. Needed to process the fact that her grandfather not only believed in ghosts but that he's spent at least two afternoons talking to one. Or at least he thought he had.

It was so different from anything she'd ever have expected from him that she lost track of time, staying up well past her normal bedtime thinking about the man she thought she'd known so well. A man who had kept secrets from her for her entire life.

Before she realized it, half the night was gone and she finally curled up on the sofa, sleeping fitfully as nightmares of ghosts hunting her kept her tossing and turning until she woke up a few hours later.

Chapter 3

Surprisingly, she felt more rested than she had in months. And now she was anxious to get back to the journals.

She fixed a pot of coffee, hauling the heavy books back out to the kitchen while it perked. Soon, she was seated with a steaming cup on her right and a napkin with two slices of buttered toast on her left. She barely touched her breakfast as she opened the one she'd been reading to where she'd left off the night before.

Working up her courage, the turned the page and there, staring back at her, was the man she'd known would be there. Apparently, a thief when he'd been alive, he'd managed to redeem himself, at least in Grandpa's eyes.

August 2, 1967

Ezra says the gold George Montgomery killed him for is still hidden somewhere on the property. He won't tell me where because he says George told others about it. Sometimes, through the years, people have come looking for it but he says they'll never find it. He's hidden it too well.

Merlin Proctor wrote of ghosts and friendships that made her wonder about his sanity. Hemisphere was weird. She got that. But was it *that* weird? Could things like this really happen? And then she knew his words must be true because in the middle of the second journal, he started writing about Hannah

Hannah, who had been her friend from early 2001 through most of 2004. Hannah, who had been very real – and closer to her than a sister might have been.

Kate didn't want to believe the words she was reading. They hurt too much and the words blurred as she read them. Hannah had been raped and murdered at the tender age of fifteen in the field behind the depot. In 1948. More than fifty years before they'd met.

December 22, 1967

I guess some of the others trust me now. I've met a few of them. William Archer is a corker. Unless Oscar Blake is around. Oscar killed William over a card game and William, understandably, is still a little ticked. And a little smug because he managed to kill Oscar a couple of years later. Unfortunately, they were both killed on the depot property so now they're stuck together for however long the curse lasts.

The one that gets me though, that makes my heart ache, is little Hannah Tremaine. I swear if there's ever any way to travel back through time, I'll find the men who did this to her and kill them myself. And it won't be quick and easy either. They'll pay dearly for hurting that sweet soul.

Yeah. Time-travel. If there ever was a way, Kate would go back and help him.

Hannah, Ezra, William, and Oscar weren't the only ghosts though. According to her grandfather the grounds were filled with them. An even dozen, all murdered somewhere on the depot property, or on the ancient, broken down train.

And because that was where they had died, violently, and because there was some sort of spell cast on the land, they were trapped there. They could leave the grounds but as soon as they did, they would disappear, only able to move around town as invisible spirits. They could also disappear while *on* the grounds, to hide from living, breathing people but when they chose to, it would be next to impossible to tell the difference between them and those who were still alive.

There were more drawings because Merle sketched all of the ghosts who resided at the depot. Beneath them, he wrote their birthdates, dates – or approximate dates – of their deaths, and who, if known, murdered them.

Ezra hadn't looked a day older when she met him yesterday than he did the day Merle drew his picture. Hannah looked the same in 1967 as she had to Kate decades later.

She traced her friend's features with a finger that trembled. Just seeing her name had been enough to make her heart ache with grief, but seeing her sweet, well-loved face brought tears to her eyes. They spilled out and ran down her cheeks.

That last summer, Hannah told her that her family was moving away. That her father had found work in another state and she had no choice but to go. They'd both cried, hugging like they were losing their best friends, because they were. They'd promised to write but Hannah said she didn't know what their address would be and though Kate waited impatiently, no letters had ever come.

Probably because dead girls had a tough time buying stationary and stamps. And what address could she have given? That of an old, abandoned depot?

Was she still there? If the words she'd read were to be believed, the answer to that question was yes. But if she was, why hadn't *she* been to one to come to her yesterday? Why Ezra and not someone she already knew and would have trusted?

Swiping at the tears, Kate jumped up from the table, grabbed her purse, and hurried out to her car. She didn't care that she'd slept in her clothes, or that she hadn't yet brushed her teeth – or her hair. She didn't care that she was driving over the speed limit, or that if there had been a cop in the area, she'd have been issued a hefty ticket. All she wanted was to get to the depot and when she did, she squealed tires turning in, kicking up a cloud of dust when she stomped on the brake and slid to a stop.

"HANNAH! WHERE ARE YOU?" she demanded, launching herself out of the car and turning in a circle. Anyone watching would have thought she'd lost her mind, spinning around, arms out to her sides as she shouted at the buildings. "Either Grandpa lied or you're here. And my grandpa never lied! *You* lied to me but *he* never did. So where are you? I've got a bone to pick with you. Show yourself!"

"I'm here," the soft voice she remembered said from behind her.

Kate whirled around, fully intending to give her the third degree, followed by a rant on how wrong it had been to say she was leaving when she never had but when she found herself staring into Hannah's bright blue eyes, all she could do was throw her arms around her, hold on like she'd never let go, and sob her heart out. Hannah just held her close, murmuring over and over that she was sorry, so sorry.

"Do you have any idea how much I missed you?" she asked later, as they sat beneath the tree where they used to have tea parties and picnics. She kept hold of her friend's hands, fearing that she might disappear before her eyes if she let go for even a second.

"Yes. I do. I missed you too, believe it or not. But Merle and I decided it was too risky to tell you the truth. You were getting older, Kate. You were changing and I just stayed the same. Physically, anyway. And when you started to notice, I got scared. You were the only girlfriend I'd had in so long I couldn't bear the thought of you thinking I was a monster. So we cooked up the story about my family moving away. It was easier than you hating me for what I was. What I am."

"I could never have hated you, Hannah. You and my grandparents were all I had. And then you were gone. I waited and waited for that letter, the one with an address so I could write you. I had such big plans for us back then." Kate laughed softly, finally letting go of one hand to reach up and wipe a few tears away. "When we graduated, we'd go to the same college, share a dorm room, party like crazy, and then get great jobs working for the same company. Later on, we'd find and marry brothers and live next door to each other. And we'd be sisters forever."

"That was a beautiful dream. I'm sorry it couldn't come true because I'd love to have been your sister," Hannah said, smiling as she wiped at her own eyes.

"You can cry?" Kate asked, then clamped her lips together. "I'm sorry. That was a really stupid question."

"No. It wasn't stupid at all. If our positions were reversed, I'd probably wonder the same thing. But yes, when we're in human form, our bodies function the same as any other human's. Something to do with whatever spell is on this place. Just because they can though, doesn't mean they have to. It's a long, complicated explanation. I don't even really understand it."

"I've got all the time in the world. I'm not going anywhere." Not this time.

Hannah seemed to think about how best to explain it and Kate waited patiently. She was just so glad to be in her friend's company again she'd have been willing to sit here for hours. It didn't matter that she was a ghost. Or that she hadn't aged a day in the past thirteen years. She was ... Hannah.

Chapter 4

"Okay," she finally said, then bit her lower lip as if unsure of what to say. "You know when you're alive – well, of course *you* do – you eat, you sleep, you use the bathroom. You *breathe*. We can do all of those things – but we don't *have* to do any of them."

"I think I understand," Kate said slowly, nodding her head. But she didn't. Not really. From the smile on Hannah's face, she knew it too.

"It's like the food. A ghost isn't going to starve to death because he or she is already dead..." The smile turned into another grin when Kate burst out laughing. "But that doesn't mean we can't enjoy a good steak or pizza."

"I wondered. You know, because you always ate the picnic stuff Grandma sent with me."

"Oh, Clara was such a wonderful cook." Hannah's eyes closed, a look of rapture falling over her face at the memories. Then she looked back at Kate. "I know you thought my family was poor. Your grandparents made sure we all had a few outfits. But they were definitely used and out of style. Merle and Clara were more concerned with making sure this place wouldn't be a burden to you someday than they were with providing us with the latest fashions. It was sweet that you wanted to make sure I ate something at least once a day. Twice, usually, because you brought enough to feed small armies."

"I hated to think that you might be hungry. You were my best friend. I've never had another who could take your place."

"I'll always be your friend," Hannah whispered, another tear zigzagging down her face.

"I wish I'd known all of this back then. Known what happened to you. I could have been a better friend. Maybe helped you in some way."

"It was over long before we ever met." The words weren't unkind, just resigned.

"Did- I mean, was there anyone here to help you through it? You were only fifteen. You must have been shattered. I know when Grandpa met you, he was so upset over it, he said if there was ever a way to travel back in time, he'd kill them before they touched you."

"Merle is such a sweetheart. I'm sure you've heard whispers about portals around Hemisphere. Portals that can let you go from one place to another in just one step. Or that there are others that let you travel through time."

"No, I guess I actually missed that bit of information," Kate said, sitting up a little straighter. "Are there really?"

"I don't know. Even fairytales are based at least a little on truth. Maybe they're there. Maybe not."

"If they did turn out to be real, would you go back? Or let someone go back and – deal with those men before they hurt you?"

Hannah was quiet for a long minute, staring off into the field across from the tracks. When she finally spoke, her words were soft, but there was no doubt she meant what she said.

"I've given a lot of thought to that possibility since I died. And no, I wouldn't. Changing history could cause a lot of problems. And what happens if the men *were* stopped? Would *I* disappear while my younger self went on to live a full life? If something didn't happen to her in later years?"

"What do you mean?"

"I mean, such as it is, I have a life that I don't think I want to give up. And much as it would have been nice to be a part of my family's life, I've still been able to visit with them. They couldn't see me because once I leave this property, I'm invisible, but I got to see my sister and brothers married. I've been able to help welcome my nieces and nephews into this world. And," she said, her tone sad, "I've attended my parents' and one brothers' funerals. They were buried next to me."

"I'm so sorry."

"It's all right. The other ghosts? They've become my family. So even if I had the chance, I wouldn't go back. I like the person I've become, even if I am stuck here forever."

"I can understand that." And she could. Sort of. "What about the men who did this to you? Were they ever caught?"

"In a manner of speaking. Two days after they killed me, they brought another girl here, intending to do the same. To rape her, to kill her, and cut off her braid like they did to me. I guess they kept the braids as a kind of trophy for each girl. I was their fourth. And, you may well hate me for this, but I wasn't going to let her be the fifth."

"I could never hate you!"

"You don't know everything about me." She was staring off into the distance, the light from the late afternoon sun casting her in a warm, golden glow.

"You can tell me anything. I promise. It won't make a difference. I'll always be your friend." After a moment, she began to speak.

"I was very angry. Very shattered, like you said. I'd just been violated in the worst way a girl could be violated. And then murdered. I didn't want to be dead, but I was. Because of them. I didn't know I was capable of that kind of rage. Of that kind of hatred. I was consumed by it. I've never despised anything or anyone as much as I did those monsters. I wanted them to pay. Ezra, William Archer, and Ben Hargrove saved the other girl. Then they tied them up and threw them in one of the sheds."

"You killed them?" Kate guessed, trying to picture Hannah as the instrument of any sort of violence. She couldn't, not really, but it wasn't difficult to imagine wanting to make them pay – with their lives. "Are they here then? As ghosts?"

"No. Oh God, no. Ezra wouldn't let me kill them until he figured out how it could be done so they died off the property. So we kept them prisoner for a day and a half." She hesitated, then took a deep breath and continued, almost as though she was reading the events from so long ago from a book. "I'm not proud of what I did then. I wasn't in my right mind. Maybe if I'd had a few weeks to adjust- I don't know. But I- I spent those hours beating on them, kicking them off and on the whole time. They were a bruised, bloody mess by the time Ezra figured out how we could do it."

"How."

"You don't want the details. Trust me."

"I'm a big girl." They stared at each other for a minute before a hint of a smile curved Hannah's lips.

"So you want all the dirt, hmm? Okay then. We stripped them of their clothes, dragged them out to the edge of the property. I took the knife they cut my hair off with, relieved them of their *manhood*, and then after letting them think about that for a minute, I cut their throats from ear-to-ear. The guys tossed them into the street so they bled to death there instead of here."

"Their *manhood?*" Hannah nodded and Kate stared at her in open-mouthed awe before bursting out laughing. "Good for you! I'd have loved to see the expressions on their faces."

"You'd have probably enjoyed them. Especially the second guy after he saw what I did to the first. They suffered because of the pain but I believe they were more horrified that they weren't 'men' anymore. Not that they ever had been, mind you. They actually begged me to kill them. I was so bitter at that point, I was almost tempted to leave them like that but figured they could still hurt and kill other girls. So they had to die."

"What a fitting end to a couple of animals. Worse than animals. Monsters," Kate said, reaching out to stroke Hannah's silky blond hair. She'd always thought she or her parents cut it because they couldn't afford a stylist. Knowing what really happened nearly broke her heart.

"You don't think less of me now? Knowing what I'm capable of?"

"Lord, no! I can't even imagine your state of mind at the time. The rage and fear... You were raped and you- You-"

"It's okay, Kate. You can say it. I was murdered. But it's okay. Eventually, I got past it and now I try not to think about it. Like I said, I'm not proud of what I did."

"You shouldn't feel bad about it though. They deserved it."

"I don't know that I feel bad, exactly. But I'm almost eighty-four years old. With the passage of time comes maturity and a realization that some of the things you did when you were younger could have maybe been handled a little differently."

"Eighty-four," Kate breathed, eyes wide as she looked at her friend. Hannah was grinning again. "You're older than Grandpa was."

"Yes, ma'am. I was almost thirteen when he was born. The funny thing is, part of me still feels the same as I did when I died."

"Do you ever leave?"

"Oh sure. It would get pretty boring if we didn't do anything but hang around here. We go to the theater all the time. Ghosts get in free, you know. Cause no one can see us after we cross the invisible line that surrounds the depot." They both laughed at that.

"That's got to be rough though, not being able to have popcorn."

"Yeah. But Merle used to bring big bags of it, along with his laptop and DVDs once those became a thing. We've actually had quite an education, at least for those who wanted to learn. Some of us spend time invading others' privacy, reading books over their shoulders, watching their television programs, learning how to use computers. And then there's Oscar. I'm not even going to say what I think he does because I could be wrong. He's a smart mouth so he might be pulling our legs." She lowered her voice to a conspiratorial tone. "The thing is, it's hard to know when he's telling the truth and when he's lying."

"He sounds charming," Kate said, her tone dripping with sarcasm.

"*No fair,*" an amused masculine voice drawled. When Kate looked around, there was no one else to be seen. "*You're giving Merle's granddaughter a bad opinion of me before we've even had a chance to meet.*"

"Forewarned is forearmed, Oscar. Now stop eavesdropping and go catch a case of fleas or something."

"*For such a sweet looking girl, you have a cruel streak, Hannah Tremaine. Cruel, I tell you.*" When she opened her mouth to rebuke him he said, "*I'm going. I'm going. But I do look forward to meeting you, Ms. Proctor.*"

"He thinks he's a lot more charming than he is. As long as you take everything he says with a grain of salt, he can be – tolerable." Kate watched her cock her head to one side, as though listening to someone else. And then she nodded and turned back to Kate. "It's getting late. Unless you want to be stuck here all night, you need to head back to the house."

Kate felt a little sick at the thought of leaving. The last time she left Hannah, it was thirteen years before she saw her again. Something in her expression must have given her away because Hannah leaned forward and wrapped her arms around her tightly.

"I'll be here tomorrow. I promise. I'm not going anywhere. Even if I wanted to, I couldn't – and I don't want to."

Kate swallowed the lump that formed in her throat and hugged her back. Hard.

"I hope not because I didn't realize how much I missed you until today. I'd gotten used to not seeing and talking to you but I guess I never got over losing my best friend."

"I'm sorry," Hannah whispered, apologizing again. "It just seemed like the only way at the time."

Chapter 5

Kate read through the rest of the first journal, which left off in the late 1970s. There were, it seemed, an even dozen ghosts on the property and her grandfather had known – and drawn – them all. It hadn't surprised her to see that the drawing of Oscar Blake was spot on based on what Hannah had told her. Almost too handsome, there was an irreverent, 'dare me' kind of look in his eyes and she definitely felt forewarned.

William Archer, on the other hand, seemed like a cute, boy next door kind of guy, though he held a grudge like nobody's business. Looks could be deceiving though. No one would ever believe he was a murderer, but he was. Granted, it was in retaliation for Oscar killing him but still- Unlike Hannah had done with her killers, William did the deed on the depot land and was now stuck having to look at Oscar's face forever.

Her dreams that night were strange. Weirder than any she could ever remember having, while at the same time bordering on frightening. Two men with pink ribbons and dresses, their voices high pitched, sang and danced in circles around her, trying to grab the ponytail she always wore. They each carried impossibly long knives. In the distance, two other men rolled and fought in the dusty parking lot and all the while, Hannah stood there telling her to run. To save herself.

When she started awake just as the sun rose above the horizon, she decided she'd had enough sleep. She crawled out of bed, slipped into her robe, then went to sit in the padded wicker chair on her narrow balcony outside her room. Both bedrooms overlooking the front yard had one while a wider, single one ran the length of the two in the back of the house.

In the distance, she could see Hampton Bay. There were already boats heading out to the open water, likely to fish. In a couple of hours, even in the chill of the early fall morning, colorful sailboats and other watercraft would start appearing. It was a peaceful way to start her day, to allow the last remnants of her dream to fade away.

She allowed her thoughts to return to yesterday, to the hours she'd spent with Hannah. She smiled remembering how nice it had been and it wasn't long before she was dressed and headed to Stan's Grocery Emporium. When she finally pulled in next to the depot, she had two large boxes of donuts and rolls, two gallons of chocolate milk, and a cooler full of sandwich fixings and sodas for lunch.

It had been close to a year since Grandpa had died and it was unlikely they'd enjoyed any food since then. She intended to see that they got plenty of it. At least until she had to go back home. Funny how, just a few short days ago, it had seemed so important to get everything settled so she could leave. Now, the thought made her sad.

"Hannah?" she called, climbing out of the car and turning in a slow circle. "I've brought breakfast. For everyone."

She couldn't help but gasp as one by one, twelve people appeared before her eyes. She'd known they were here. Or at least some part of her brain accepted that they were. But to see them in the flesh, materializing out of thin air, was a bit of a shock.

"Don't freak out," Ezra said quietly, coming to stand on her left. Hannah, she noted, was on her right. Kate hadn't even seen them move. "They won't hurt you."

"He's right," Hannah told her. "Just take a few slow breaths. You're white as a ghost."

One of the women started to laugh but slapped a hand over her mouth. More snickers followed, and soon all of them were nearly doubled over with laughter. Kate couldn't deny the humor in her friend's observation and finally began to laugh too.

"All right," she said, after a couple of minutes passed. "Do you guys want to haul this stuff out of my car? I've brought breakfast and lunch. I figured I'd see what you all want for supper before I pick that up."

Her grandparents' insurance policies were very generous so she could easily feed them – indefinitely. And in case she ever ran out of that, there were the stacks of hundred dollar bills. She'd yet to count it but knew it would add up to tens of thousands of dollars. Maybe hundreds.

"Thank you. For doing this," Ezra said, flashing her a shy grin once they were all seated beneath the oak tree. "Like Hannah said, we won't starve to death but food still tastes good and it's nice to have it again."

"You're welcome."

She wasn't sure what else to say as she watched the gentle giant work his way through four cinnamon rolls and two big glasses of milk. He must have been six-four if he was an inch. A big hulk of a man, yet both times they'd spoken, his voice was gentle and respectful. Combined with a face that would make Hollywood moguls sit up and take notice, she figured he must have been popular with the ladies back in the day.

Lost in thought, she didn't notice when everyone but Ezra and Hannah wandered away. When she next became aware of her surroundings, they were all standing in the distance, pretending to be busy talking to one another but she could tell they were paying close attention to what was happening under the tree. She also noted that Oscar and William were throwing pointed looks at Ezra. Eventually, he cleared his throat. Then he cleared it again.

"I- Uh- *We* have a proposition we'd like to make," he said, looking her straight in the eye before glancing down at the hands he'd folded in front of him.

"Okay..." Kate waited for another long minute before he continued.

"We were talking about this with Merle, before he was killed last year. Actually, it was his idea. He was going to talk to you about it but, well, he never got the chance." He looked up at her again. "A lot of old depots around the world have been turned into restaurants. This place is big and it wouldn't really take much to fix it up."

"There's also the train," Hannah said, excitement making her face light up. "A lot of them have dinner trains. And then there's the hotel over there..." She glanced at Ezra, waiting for him to take over again.

"There are twelve of us. We don't require sleep. We don't get sore muscles from working too hard. We've learned a lot over the years."

"I know. Hannah told me."

"So what we propose is this. We fix up both buildings and the train. Then we work in all of them, cooking, cleaning, whatever needs done. You get free labor, one hundred percent of the profits, and what we believe will be a thriving business. And all you have to do is buy the supplies we need to get everything fixed up and ready to go."

Chapter 6

Twelve Ghosts Bar & Grill
The Eerie Eatery & Pub
Sleep With the Dead Hotel
Ghostly's Gastronomical Grub and Cups
Bewitching Brews & Chews

The ideas had come pouring in as twelve ghosts worked hard to convince her that this was a great idea. Instead of busting her butt to make another restaurant owner wealthy, *they* would bust theirs to make her rich. All they asked in return was cable TV, a fast internet connection, and a few computers.

Kate paced back and forth, from one end of the house to the other. Sometimes up and down the stairs. Her thoughts were a jumbled, almost panicked mess.

She had a life back in Chicago. A job she'd started working at when she was fifteen. An apartment. Even her parents, such as they were. Some part of them must still care for her, and someday they might forgive her. It was a long shot, but anything was possible.

Here, she had what? A big house with happy memories – and an acre and a half of property filled with bored out of their minds ghosts.

A restaurant? Based on Hemisphere's big yearly festival? Run by ghosts who had been murdered by humans and monsters alike. If she could believe all of the stories. Ben Hargrove claimed to have been killed by a vampire. The two holes on the side of his neck were proof of that, he claimed and Kate couldn't think of anything else that might have caused them. But- *A vampire?*

"This is nuts," she muttered, stopping at the front window to look out at the dark. The only light came from streetlights that seemed to be spaced too far apart and a few stars that managed to peek out from behind the thick cloud cover.

There were ghosts in Hemisphere. She knew that for a fact. But were there also monsters? Blood sucking vampires – and worse? Was that why her grandparents always insisted she not go out after dark? Why they always insisted that a salt line be poured across each doorway and windowsill?

"And I'm actually considering opening businesses here..."

And she was. What other option was there? She couldn't just abandon Hannah to more decades, maybe centuries, of tedium. Sure, she could keep the property, pay the tax and insurance on it, continue hiring someone to mow and keep the weeds and grass down so she didn't get fines from the city. Maybe even keep power turned on in one of the buildings so they could entertain themselves with television and internet. But they'd still be bored.

"I'm worried about ghosts having a purpose? I need to be locked up somewhere," she muttered, shaking her head at the craziness of her thoughts.

Feeling a little creeped out, Kate closed the drapes to shut the world out. She'd always heard about towns that rolled up the streets at six but had never seen it anywhere but here. An occasional vehicle would drive past but for all intents and purposes, when the sun set, the day was done in Hemisphere. Except for things and creatures that owned the night. And those brave enough to venture out with them.

After checking the salt lines throughout the house, Kate headed for the bathroom, turned the shower to steamy hot, stripped, then stepped into the tub to stand under the spray.

Nice.

She didn't know whether the voice in her head was real, or if she was just jumpy and suspicious after the things Hannah had told her but she opened her eyes, looked around, slid the shower door open a bit and said,

"I swear, Oscar, if you're invading *my* privacy, I'll find an exorcist and you'll be gone from here and the depot so fast it'll make your head spin."

It might have been her imagination but the creepy feeling that had been so strong lessened a bit. She wasn't going to worry about it though. Instead, she allowed the heat from the water to relax muscles that had tensed at the first suggestion of opening the depot for business.

She wondered what some of the people she knew back home would say if she ran this scenario by them, then laughed. They'd be petitioning someone to have her admitted for a psych evaluation as soon as possible. Even if they believed her, they'd tell her it wasn't her job to take care of a bunch of dead people.

The only problem was, her grandfather had cared. Enough, in fact, that he'd introduced her to one of them. A ghost she'd come to love as much as a sister. A ghost she'd *always* love like a sister. So she couldn't just walk away. She'd never do that to Hannah.

She'd have a hard time doing that to any of them though. Spending so much time with her grandparents as she was growing up, she'd learned to feel compassion for those less fortunate. Most of these 'people' would qualify, especially Hannah and the other three women, who had died under similar circumstances.

Unable to work up an interest for the journals, Kate headed to bed early, then tossed and turned most of the night. Again, her dreams were beyond weird, with just a hint of danger thrown in. Danger that felt very real, even as her brain was telling her the rest of it was laughable.

But at least when she woke dark and early in the morning, she thought she might have come up with a solution. Open everything the way they wanted, leave Hannah in charge, and just come back a few times a year to make sure everything was running smoothly.

Jed, her boss, would extend her vacation. She had six more weeks and if it took longer than that, he'd let her have more, though it would be unpaid.

She spent most of the morning on her laptop, working out a tentative schedule and business plan. With ghosts who didn't tire out, they could work round the clock, and they'd do it for two reasons. First, because they *were* bored out of their minds and needed something to occupy themselves and second, because she'd keep them supplied with all manner of food. For dead people, they sure loved to eat.

"WE WERE AFRAID WE'D scared you off," Ezra said, his voice, as always, quiet when he opened her car door.

"No. I just had to do some thinking. Some planning. And I think I've figured everything out. If you all agree to it anyway." She held up her laptop. "Can you get everyone together. I'll head inside."

She didn't have much choice with the chilly drizzle that had been falling all morning. She'd never spent much time in Hemisphere in the fall because school started in early September so she was surprised to find the term 'rainy season' could easily apply here. At least it could this year.

By the time everyone gathered, she had the computer set up on the rickety ice cream counter and let them look through the files she'd created. She could hear them talking softly amongst themselves as she wandered around the empty, cavernous room.

In her mind, she was seeing the changes she wanted made. The spotless, intimately lit dining room, the clean and bright kitchen area. Sparkling windows with pristine....

"The Cream-a-torium!" William whooped, laughing uproariously. "That's fantastic!"

Kate grinned at his delight at the name for the ice cream parlor. The seemed to be pleased with her other choices as well. Twelve Ghosts Pub & Grill, The Haunted Dinner Train, and the Rest-Inn-Peace.

"Seven weeks isn't a lot of time," Ben murmured. She watched him scroll through the next few screens. "Of course, with the dozen of us working three shifts a day, that's actually twenty-one weeks in human time, or about five months. Yeah. I think we can do it. As long as you can keep us in building materials and equipment."

"Then shall we try to firm up these plans?" Kate asked, rejoining the group. "I'd like to hear where you think we should start first."

"We need to get everything cleaned," Annabelle Morgan said firmly, hands on her curvaceous hips as she surveyed the room.

"Electricity," William added. "We'll need to be able to see what we're doing and it's too dark in here without an adequate source of light. Besides, it would be nice to listen to some music while we're working."

"Good ideas. We can figure out the rest as we go along," Kate said, nodding her approval. "I'll call the power company. It'll probably be a few days but I can pick up some pretty powerful rechargeable flashlights. We'll have to work in small areas but at least we can get started, right?"

"Well what are you waiting for?" Hannah asked, laughing as she threw her arms around Kate. "Go get the stuff. And *thank you!* Thank you *so* much!"

"You're welcome," Kate whispered, blinking back the tears that filled her eyes.

It was going to be hard to leave her when everything was ready but at least this time, she'd know where to find her. And they wouldn't have to go even a day without some sort of contact. Phone, texts, emails, Skype. For as long as Kate lived, Hannah would be here and always be her friend.

"I don't mean to be Johnny Raincloud," Ezra said, coming to stand beside them, "but if I were you, I'd pick up some mouse and rat traps, and whatever you use in this day and age for bugs."

"Um- Did you say- Did you say *rat traps?*" Kate asked, her voice barely above a whisper as she glanced around the floor making sure there were no rodents near her. She hoped Ezra was strong because if she saw one, she would be jumping into his arms so fast it might make his head spin.

"Unfortunately, yes." When she looked at him, it was clear he was fighting to control a smile. She could see hints of dimples wanting to appear when he spoke again. "Merle used to put stuff out to control them but it's been almost a year and they're making a comeback."

"Yes. Yes, *of course* I'll get something for the – pests!"

She was also going to get some knee high rubber boots and some thick work gloves because she wasn't going to risk one running across her feet, up a pant leg, or on her hands. If there was anything Kate hated, it was creepy crawlies and there was no way she'd allow her name to be associated with them. Ghosts, yes. There was no getting around that. But bugs and other critters? No way.

By the time she returned from the home improvement store with enough cleaning supplies, traps, and poisons to take care of the Empire State Building, it was clear her new *employees* were one-hundred percent serious about wanting to make this venture pay. They'd already piled everything that wasn't nailed down in the depot in one of the empty sheds between there and the hotel.

Ezra and Pete Madison managed to find some sad excuses for brooms and were kicking up a dust cloud inside as they swept from the east end of the building to the west. William, Ben, Henry Babett and, surprisingly, Oscar, grabbed the four wide push brooms she'd picked up.

The ladies would have started with the mopping but when they turned the faucets in the kitchen sink on, nothing came out. Kate made a quick call to the city to have that taken care of and was surprised when they said they could have it on the next day.

It would take three before the power company could get there. She'd had some reservations about electricity running through old wires and outlets but Oscar claimed to know how to check everything to make sure it was safe. She hoped she wasn't wrong in believing him.

"There's lots we can do between now and tomorrow," Hannah told her, locking elbows and leading her toward the hotel. "You don't need to be in all that dust. It won't affect us at all but it could make you sick. We can get the hotel cleared out and swept too. You'll have to rent a couple of big dumpsters at some point after we get everything out but there should be enough shed storage to last us a while. Hey, buddy," she said, squatting down to pet a scruffy looking dog. Like the ghosts were able to do, it seemed to appear from nowhere. "Say hello to Kate." She glanced up, smiling her encouragement. "It's okay. He won't hurt you. He's been coming here off and on for a few years now. I keep hoping he'll be adopted by a good family but if he has been, he still finds his way back to us for visits."

The dog whined a little and Kate reached out a hand, reluctantly, for it to sniff. She'd bet the thing hadn't had a bath in months and without soap and water, she really didn't want to touch it. But when she finally gave in, she was surprised at how soft his fur was.

"You're a good boy, aren't you," she said like she was talking to an infant.

"You'll have to go lie down for now," Hannah told him after a couple of minutes. "We've got work to do but we'll have snacks for you later. I promise."

Chapter 7

Over the next seven days, to say the depot underwent a major transformation would have been an understatement. From dark, dirty, and smelling faintly of mold and mildew to squeaky clean with fresh white primer covering all of the walls. The ceiling and rafters had been covered in a high gloss brown paint and just because they could, dozens of strings of white lights had been hung from end to end, creating a starry sky effect.

It was breathtakingly beautiful during the day and Kate wished she could see it after dark. Unfortunately, this was Hemisphere and Hannah and Ezra made sure she was headed home well before sunset. One day though, she vowed, she would just bring a sleeping bag and spend the night.

But that was low on the list of things that needed to be done. While the ghosts worked around the clock – literally – she spent her waking hours pricing booths, tables, chairs, and kitchen equipment for the depot. She also spent countless hours scouring the internet for train parts but that was proving to be a major headache. The most important thing she did though, in her opinion, was finding where to get everything they'd need to furnish thirteen guest rooms and the small apartment behind the registration desk.

Since they wouldn't need to hire anyone once it was up and running, she wanted the ghosts to have the apartment. They thought she should turn it into a couple of extra rooms but Kate refused. They hadn't had any sort of *real* home in forever and this was one thing she could do for them. Once it was finished, they'd have a place to relax, watch television, and play on her computer.

They'd set up a fair schedule for taking turns on it but, from what she could gather, the only one who used it for anything other than bringing up music was Oscar. He was probably browsing all of the porn sites. If he was though, he was deleting the evidence. She could be wrong. If she was, it would be a surprise.

What was shocking was seeing how hard he worked. And the fact that he seemed to know everything there was to know about all things mechanical. He'd already fixed the ancient furnace and installed a new central air system, an on demand hot water heater, and a commercial dishwasher.

He, along with everyone else, really was working around the clock, busting their butts each day while she was there. But what they always managed to accomplish after she headed home, while she lay sleeping the hours away at her grandparents' house, just astounded her. In less than three weeks, they'd made countless repairs. Some, like the wiring and plumbing, had to wait until permits had been issued but they found other ways to occupy themselves. By the time the rest of the kitchen equipment, booths, and tables arrived, they were going to be more than ready to set it all up.

Two nights later, the shed, nearly overflowing with debris, caught fire. When she got the call, Kate didn't even bother changing out of the lounge pants and tank top she wore instead of pajamas. She just grabbed her purse and ran for the car. It never even occurred to her that she'd just broken one of her grandparent's rules. She was out after dark.

When she arrived, firemen were doing everything in their power to contain the blaze, to keep it from spreading to the hotel. Except for the roof, doorways, and window frames, the depot was all brick and not in much danger but the hotel was completely combustible and everyone worried it might burn to the ground as the old wood crackled and sparked, sending showers of glowing embers high into the air.

"You shouldn't be out here," Ezra said, his tone calm yet firm.

"I'm fine." But she wasn't. This place had been too important to her grandfather, contained too many memories to risk losing. He'd worked so hard to keep the secrets, to protect the ghosts. She couldn't bear it if it all came to ruin under her watch.

"Kate, there's too much smoke. Wait in the depot. You can watch from the windows." He put a gentle hand in the middle of her back, intending to guide her to safety but she didn't move, just stood there, staring at the mesmerizing orange and yellow flames as they danced and soared, reaching ever outward for anything they might consume. She felt his arm move to her shoulders, his free hand wrapping around her arm, tugging her in the direction of safety. "Kate, let's go. Annabelle is making coffee."

She glanced up, into his kind brown eyes, and just melted against his side. She might not know him well but he was always nice, always considerate, and always seemed to be looking out for her. He might have been a train robber when he was alive but she'd have bet he was a gentleman, even then.

"*Kate!*" He shook her gently, then leaned down from his towering height to peer into her face. "Let's get some coffee."

"All right," she finally murmured, glancing once more at the blaze, then walking with him into the now bright and cheerful depot.

Hannah met them at the door, taking one of her hands and Ezra's arm dropped away, though he followed them to a folding table set up near the kitchen. Without his warmth, and surprisingly, the ghosts were all warm, her shoulders felt cold and she shivered a little.

"William is making breakfast," Hannah told her. "And you will eat, Kate. No arguments."

No arguments. Not when it was a dozen to one and they'd all nag her until she did as they demanded. It wouldn't be a hardship though. William, it seemed, had learned a lot by hovering over the shoulders of the best cooks and chefs in Hemisphere. Practicing for a few hours each day, he was turning out amazing meals for everyone to ooh and ahh over.

This morning though, Kate barely tasted the perfectly golden hash browns, eggs, sausage, and toast he set before her. She was tired. The night had been too short and when she finished less than half of what was on her plate, she put her arms on the tabletop, laid her head down, and fell asleep.

IT TOOK A MOMENT TO figure out that she wasn't lying in her bed at her grandparents' house. In fact, when it finally registered where she was, she could hardly breathe. A chest. A man's solid chest – and she was sprawled against it like she slept there all the time. Like she was used to the pair of strong arms that held her close.

"Hannah thought you'd be more comfortable like this than bent over the table." Ezra... She was plastered against Ezra like she belonged there.

Her memories fuzzy because she hadn't woken up completely yet, combined with her current proximity to a dead guy, made her forget all about the fire – for about ten seconds.

"The shed!" she gasped, sitting straight up, her hands pressed against him to keep her balance. "The hotel-"

"The hotel is fine. The shed's almost out now," Ezra reassured her quickly.

"And the best part of all," Oscar said from where he sat cross-legged on the floor on the other side of the wide dining area, "is that you won't need a dumpster for that mess now. Or not much of one. Most of it is gone now. Win/win, if you ask me."

"No one asked you," Hannah snapped, rolling her eyes heavenward. "But it will save you a little money," she conceded after a moment.

"Um... Do they know what caused it?"

"Arson," Ezra said, getting to his feet and helping Kate to hers when it became obvious she was getting up.

"Thanks," she murmured, not quite able to meet his eyes. Ezra cleared his throat before continuing. "How?"

"They found a couple of charred gas cans inside. Since we didn't throw anything like that away, it had to have been set deliberately."

"Who would have done something like that?" she asked, walking to the window closest to the charred shed. Smoke rose from the rubble. "It's just an old, abandoned depot. We're not even in a prime business location so the land isn't that valuable."

"Maybe a restaurant owner in town is worried that we'll be too much competition," Ben suggested from close by. Kate glanced over her shoulder to see him standing beside her, staring out at the mess outside. "Maybe they're trying to scare us off."

"It won't work," she said softly, then louder, "It won't work."

"No," Ezra agreed. "It won't. But from now on, one of us will be keeping an eye out at all times so nothing like this happens again."

Half an hour later, the fire marshal came inside. He apologized to Kate saying that while there was no question it was arson, it was doubtful they'd ever know who set the fire. The only evidence had been tossed in the shed, meaning any fingerprints were gone. And given the location of the property, it was unlikely there had been any witnesses.

"Thank you," she told him. There wasn't much else to say but she could let him know she appreciated their hard work. "For saving the rest of the buildings." The man turned a little red but nodded once.

"Do you have insurance on it?" he asked.

"Yes." But she wouldn't file a claim. They had been planning on tearing that shed down anyway and the last thing she needed was to risk higher premiums at this stage of the game.

"That's good. We'll have the report written up by the end of the day."

"Thank you again."

"It could be worse," William said, watching as the men who spent half the night and most of the morning putting out the fire climb back on board the trucks.

"Yes. It could be," Kate agreed. Much, much worse. But knowing someone deliberately set the fire was a little nerve racking.

"You don't sound like you believe it."

"Oh, I do. We could have lost the hotel. Or the supplies we've got stored in the other shed."

"Then why are you so down?" Hannah asked, coming to stand beside her. "We were going to tear it all down and throw everything away anyway."

"Maybe I watch too many crime dramas but I can only assume someone was trying to send us a message."

"Or maybe it was just a couple of young punks who had too much to drink and thought this would be a fun way to pass the time." This suggestion came from Oscar.

"And that's something you'd know a lot about, isn't it?" William asked, unable to keep the harshness out of his tone. "Ruining things, like people's lives and livelihood."

"Are we going to keep rehashing this?" Oscar snapped, glaring at him. "You cheated, I killed you, get over it. It was more than eighty years ago. And *you* killed me too. *Remember?* That should make you happy."

"What would have made me happy is if I'd killed you on the other side of the property line."

"Well you didn't-"

"Enough!" Annabelle said, clapping her hands sharply. "You need to let it go, William. We were all murdered. Now we're stuck for eternity – or however long the spell lasts. So if you can't kiss and make up, then just shut up about it. You've nursed this grudge for too long and I, for one, am beyond tired of hearing about it!" With that, she flounced off to the kitchen area.

"I'm pretty tired of it too," Oscar told him. "And for your information, I've never been guilty of arson in my life."

"No, you're just guilty of being a pervert and a porn addict."

"Says *you*. You all just assume that's what I do. You have no proof."

"Well, you *were* watching me in the shower," Kate reminded him, rolling her eyes heavenward.

"You were what?" Ezra demanded, his voice low as he crossed the room to join them.

"What?" Oscar asked, and she would have sworn he looked shocked at her accusation. "While I'm sure it would be well worth the effort, I haven't paid a visit to Merle and Clara's since before Merle was killed."

"And we can believe everything that comes out of your mouth." Clearly, William wasn't ready to let bygones be bygones.

"Believe whatever you want but if someone was watching Kate, it wasn't me." He was telling the truth. She could tell by the look in his eyes.

"Who could it have been then?" she demanded, a chill working its way down her spine and making her shiver.

"Or *what?*"

"Another ghost?" Hannah asked. Clearly, she believed him too.

"Maybe. Or maybe someone who has the power to disappear when they want to."

"Have you been putting out the salt lines?" Ezra demanded, looking more than a little concerned.

"Yes. Maybe. I – might have forgotten a couple of times."

Chapter 8

Not once, as far back as she could remember, had Kate ever been afraid to walk into her grandparent's house. But she was today. Even staring at the three, twenty pound bags of finely ground salt she'd picked up at the Hemisphere Sodium Co-op, she was more frightened than she'd ever been in her life. Hands shaking, she took out her cell phone and called the depot. Ezra answered on the first ring.

"I'm here. Inside the house," she told him, trying to sound more confident than she felt.

"Okay, good. I know it's not much comfort but everyone is with you but me. They'll let me know if you need to hit any areas better and then I'll tell you. All right?"

"Okay."

"All right now. Head up to the attic and start flinging."

Heart in her throat, Kate did what he said. Over the next two hours, she flung more salt than she ever wanted to see again. Every now and again, Ezra would tell her she needed to hit a spot with a little more but before the sun went down, she'd salted every square foot of the house, sending it up in the air first.

By the time she'd worked herself to the front door, the ghosts declared her house a spirit-free zone – and that included them because they were now relegated to the yard and front porch. In a couple of days, she could vacuum the floors and furniture, as long as she remembered to keep the salt lines across the doors and window sills – and made sure nothing broke them. Ever.

"I'm still scared," she whispered, not wanting to hang up and break the connection.

"I know. But you've got wall-to-wall salt now. If there was anything in there, you either sent it to its maker or it had to leave too. We'll guard the yard around the house as best we can and someone will always have the phone here. At the very least, we can get 911 heading your way in a hurry." She could hear the frustration in his voice over their limitations in protecting her. "One way or another, we'll keep you safe. You have my word."

You have my word.

Something in that phrase sounded familiar, enough so that over the next few hours, she tried to remember why. It didn't help. Whatever it was hovered at the edges of her mind but she couldn't pull it forward enough to make it a coherent thought.

At ten, she gave up on trying to summon a memory that didn't want to be found, crawled into bed, tucked the handgun under her pillow, and held the phone to her chest like the lifeline she now considered it to be. After only the slightest of hesitations, she dialed the depot.

"What's happening?" Ezra demanded. There was little doubt that her call had shaken him, made him worry even more.

"Nothing. I- I'm just lying here trying to fall asleep and I can't. I keep thinking that a bad – I don't know – ghost or spirit was in here spying on me and-" She didn't even want to put the fear she still felt into words.

"You're afraid, Kate. Under the circumstances, that's normal." His voice went from being on alert to soft and gentle. Soothing, she thought, closing her eyes and listening to the deep timbre so familiar to her now. "Remember, you've got half a dozen ghosts stationed around the perimeter of your house." The rest were still guarding the depot property. "Nothing and no one is going to get by them. And if they do, someone can be here in seconds so I can call the police."

She didn't know how long he talked to her after he changed the subject and started talking about everything under the sun. Ben and

Annabelle flirting a little more when they thought no one was looking. William and his incessant nagging that everything must be perfect and thinking aloud about the menu he wanted to serve once Twelve Ghosts was up and running.

And then the sun was up and Kate couldn't get out of the house fast enough. She wondered if her guards would follow her, then remembered Ezra telling her they'd always have four there, keeping an eye out, making sure no human could get in without them knowing about it. And that's all they were making sure of now since spirits or other undead creatures wouldn't be able to get past the salt.

It took a few days but slowly, she began to feel safe at the house again. Or safer. The fact that she'd had an intruder though was always at the back of her mind. And in her dreams. Always in her dreams, stalking her, watching her. No matter how early she went to bed, she never woke feeling rested.

By the time she pulled onto the property nearly a week later, she was exhausted – and in no mood to deal with whatever everyone was waiting to tell her. Except they didn't say a word. Ezra just nodded toward the depot. No one else, not even Hannah, would meet her eyes. And so, after a fortifying breath, she walked purposefully to the door, opened it, and stepped inside.

Go away or die, ghost lover. Hemisphere doesn't need your kind.

Big red letters had been sprayed on the wall directly across from the doors. Streaks of paint had rolled down from words like blood from a wound, marring the fresh coat of cream colored paint that had barely had time to dry.

"They used a comma," she murmured, wondering if she'd gone over some sort of edge. She was looking at a death threat – a death threat directed at her – and what stood out most was that the graffiti artist used correct punctuation.

"Yeah. I noticed that too," Ben said, coming to stand on her left, wrapping an arm around her shoulders. Ezra was on her right, with everyone else gathered around her like her own personal Secret Service detail. "I'd just like to know how they got past us." Him and everyone else in the room, Kate thought, scowling at the words on the wall.

"We can't protect you when you leave here," Ezra told her, his voice soft but serious. Like he expected her to heed whatever he said. "We don't know who's doing this. We don't know if this is an idle threat or if they mean business but-"

"But if they do, they can kiss my foot." Kate felt a wave of anger—of tsunami proportions – surge through her. "Grandpa left this to *me*. It's mine. It's *ours!* And I'm not going to be pushed out. I'm finished being scared. I'm not leaving." She pulled away from Ben, turned in a slow circle, her eyes darting everywhere.

"Kate-" Ezra tried to stop her, probably to finish his lecture but she pulled away from him too.

"Did you hear that?" she demanded, her tone just shy of a shout. "Whatever your plan was, it just backfired. I'm not leaving Hemisphere. Ever. I'm going to call and quit my job today. I'm not even going to go back to pack. I'll have some friends do it and ship my stuff to me. So whoever you are, you better get used to my face because you're going to be seeing a lot of it!"

"Then you need to stay here," Ezra told her, and from his tone, she knew he wouldn't be listening to any arguments. "We weren't going to start on the hotel until we were finished here but we'll put if off until we can get the manager's apartment ready. That should only take a few days. In the meantime, you'll have to toss down here in a sleeping bag or bedroll. We'll keep guards on you round the clock."

"I'm not going to stay here like a trapped animal," she pointed out. "I have a life to live, supplies to pick up."

"Then we'll keep sending three of us to guard you. One will tag along to make sure no one messes with the car and the other two will go wherever you are. If something happens, one of them will get back to me and I'll call you."

IT DIDN'T TAKE LONG to return to the house, pack her bags, the journals, the money, and hunt up her grandfather's camping equipment. He'd done a good job of packing everything in plastic bins – with dryer sheets, no less – so everything smelled fresh. She grabbed both sleeping bags and an inflatable mattress. Might as well be comfortable, she thought, packing everything in the car. Then she ran in to collect the perishables from the refrigerator. Everything else could wait.

It wasn't long before she was back at the depot, pitching in to help cover the graffiti, and then moving on to the next job. The floors would be next on the list and she worked side-by-side with the ghosts laying the tile that had been delivered from the home improvement store a few days ago.

Ben, the self-appointed foreman for the group, kept calling for breaks, ten minutes every hour, and Kate knew it was because of her. As the only live human, she was the only one who got tired and sore. It was sweet that they were so concerned about her welfare.

They seemed to love having a purpose in life again too and she never heard a word of complaint. Frequent debates over the right way to do a job, and the occasional argument, yes, but complaints? Not a single one.

Hard working ghosts...

A month ago, she'd have never believed it. Not in ghosts and certainly not that she'd be working alongside them to open a restaurant and hotel.

A few days after her move to the depot, as she laid on the air mattress, snuggled into one of the sleeping bags, Kate found she couldn't sleep. She tried not to think of the major changes she'd made in her life after seeing the threat. Quitting a job she'd worked at almost half her life. Moving to a city she'd only spent vacations in. A city where she had no family now. Just a bunch of dead people she'd befriended.

In an effort to stop the thoughts, to stave off the panic she could feel begin in the pit of her stomach, she picked up the journal she'd left off in after learning about Hannah.

From day to day, much of what her grandfather wrote about was the same and she found herself skimming a lot of it. Until she got to the part where he'd met and married Cora, her much loved grandma. She read about her father, what a good little boy he'd been but how he'd fallen in with a bad crowd in high school. Then he married and Kate had been born and Merle and Cora worried themselves sick that their granddaughter was being raised by drug addicts.

Then she got to the year she turned six and the words began to blur before her tear filled eyes and she started to shake. Not just a slight tremble but shaking like she'd been too long in the cold.

She'd known about them. Twenty-two years ago, *she'd known*. And it had, apparently, been more than her little girl brain could handle and she'd blocked it all out. But her grandpa had told her everything and, if his words were to be believed, it had been in hopes that she'd do pretty much what she was doing right now. Giving up her life to help his precious ghosts.

"It's not what you're thinking," Ezra said quietly. When she looked up, he was sitting cross-legged beside her on the mattress. The same way he'd been sitting that day. She hadn't thought of him in all that time but now she remembered that.

"I know you," she whispered, looking up at him from her pillow, wishing she could sink into it, fall asleep and then pretend it was all a dream. Again. "I talked to you when I was a little girl."

"Yes, we talked. I've always wished I could apologize to you after the nightmares. I – we – never meant to scare you."

"He – wanted me to take care of you."

"I don't know if it was that as much as to make sure you never sold the depot. We don't know what would happen to us if it ever left your family's ownership."

"Did he ever care about anyone like he did all of you?" Did he ever really love *her*?

"He never loved anyone as much as he did you and your grandma."

"He- He said Hannah was Plan B. I'm assuming it was so I'd care enough to take over for him, here, after he and Grandma were gone."

"It wasn't just for them, Katie."

Her breath caught when she heard the voice behind her. So familiar, so loved, so missed. It couldn't be. Could it? She looked at Ezra, who looked as stunned as she felt. He shook his head in answer to her unspoken question, then he smiled tenderly at her before he faded away to nothing.

And then the man who'd always done his best to take care of her was there, kneeling beside the bed, holding her close when she threw herself off the mattress and into his arms. If anyone had seen her, both here and at his funeral, they'd probably have said she cried harder now than she had then. And they'd probably be right.

Then, she'd only hurt because she didn't know how she'd face the rest of her life without him in it. Now, she'd experienced what that life would be like and it had been hard. One of the hardest things she'd ever had to adjust to. Except she hadn't really adjusted, just learned to bury the pain.

"How?" she asked, a long while later, still unable to let him go.

"I was murdered here, sweetheart. I'm just as bound by whatever spell was placed on this land as everyone else."

"Why did you wait so long to let me know you were here?" The better question, she thought, was why hadn't she realized he'd have to be here too?

"I didn't want you to decide to stay because of me. You needed to decide for yourself whether you wanted to be here or not, if you wanted to be friends with the ghosts." Merle was stroking her hair softly, his words gentle as he held her to his chest, just as he'd done when she'd cried all those years ago.

"But- I quit my job a few days ago. I'd already decided to stay."

"You made that decision in the heat of the moment, because you were mad and scared. You might have changed your mind."

"If I'd known you were here, I'd have never changed my mind. Never." Not if she could have him in her life again.

"I know, baby." She did pull away then, looking up at him, surprised by the anger that surged up in her.

"Then you know how much I missed you. How alone I felt. How I would have given anything – *anything* – to see you again. To talk to you again." To not be alone anymore.

"Katie," he said, reaching out to stroke her cheek. "If what you really wanted was to be done with Hemisphere, with the depot, I didn't want to hold you back. I knew you'd do the right thing. Make sure they were all safe, but until I knew for sure you *wanted* to be here, I couldn't take a chance on tying you to a dead man."

"It should have been my choice, Grandpa," she accused, but there was no real censure in her voice now. She was too glad to see him again.

"Maybe. I don't know. I just didn't want to be the one to force you to give up a life you loved for one you only settled for because of me." Merle pulled her into another hug and she didn't resist.

"You're my family, Grandpa. Mom and Dad don't care. Just you and Grandma." Her heart sped up for a moment. "Is- Is she here too?" She felt more than heard his sigh.

"I wish she was, sweetie, but she died in the hospital. She's not kept here because of the spell. Or curse. No one really knows what it is."

"Well whatever it is, I'm glad. It kept you here. And I didn't give up a life I loved. I gave up one I was used to. One that felt safe because I had the job. Now I'll get to have my own restaurant – and keep a hundred percent of the profits, right, Ezra?" She heard his chuckle and smiled.

"You're sure this is what you want then?"

"I was pretty sure before. Now I *am* sure. I should have moved here after graduation." Or at the very least, after her grandmother got sick.

"No regrets, sweetheart," Merle murmured. "Hindsight is twenty-twenty, kiddo. We can't change what we could have or should have done in the past. We can only move forward with what we know today."

"Well today, I know we're together – and I'm not going away again. I know we've got a restaurant to get in shape. And I know we're being watched by a dozen ghosts who are eavesdropping on us." She heard a jumble of giggles and laughter. "Come on out, everyone. We've got some celebrating to do."

"Welcome back, Merle. I'll make us all a snack," William declared, appearing first and thumping him on the back. His grin was contagious. "I've been wanting to try out a recipe for gourmet salted caramel and dark chocolate popcorn." He walked toward the kitchen, stocked – at the moment – only with a microwave, a couple electric burners, and a toaster oven, muttering to himself.

One by one, the other ghosts appeared, slapping Merle on the back or hugging him, welcoming him back to the depot.

"We wondered if the spell ended when Cynthia was killed back in '97," Ben said, looking as pleased as Kate had ever seen him. "Or we thought maybe it only applied to a dozen of us."

"No. I've been here all along. I just wanted my Katie to make up her own mind and I know none of you can keep a secret." Ben threw his head back and laughed.

"Yeah. It would have been a tough one to keep from that granddaughter of yours." He finally stepped aside to let Ezra in.

"You know I'm going to kick your butt, right?" he asked as Merle got to his feet. They wrapped their arms around each other in a bear hug Kate thought might never end. "I missed you, you old coot."

"I missed you too, older coot than me." He slapped Merle on the back, then laughed and said, "It's a good thing we haven't had the sign and menus made yet because we're going to have to change the name of the restaurant to Thirteen Ghosts now."

"That has a nice ring to it," Merle agreed, smiling at Kate. "If it's all right with my granddaughter."

"I think it's perfect," she told him, blinking away a few more tears.

And then everyone was talking and laughing and it sounded like there were about fifty people in the room instead of fourteen. No matter how many improvements they'd made over the past few weeks, no matter that everyone seemed happy enough, the appearance of her grandfather made everything seem brighter. Like he'd been the missing link and now that he was here, everything was right.

At least it was for Kate. For the first time in almost a year, *she* was happy again. And she looked forward to the future. To a future with her grandpa, with her best friend, and eleven other ghosts she was coming to care for more than she'd ever have believed possible.

THANKS SO MUCH FOR reading The Depot, Book 2 in Haunted Depot: The Ghost Curse. I hope you enjoyed Kate's story. And that you'll leave a review letting others know. Word of mouth not only helps readers who might love the story find it, but it also helps those who might not to pass it by.

And don't forget to sign up for the Hemisphere Orientation and New Resident's Packet to find out more insider secrets about our unique little town.

Keep reading for a free offer and news about new releases.

Thanks again,

Kristy

Other Works by Kristy K. James

Coach's Boys Series
The Daddy Pact, Book 1
A Hero for Holly, Book 2
A Harry Situation, Book 3
Her Best Friend Jon, Book 4
Code Red Christmas, Book 5
Darby's Dilemma, Book 6
The Detective's Second Chance, Book 7
Back to the Beginning, Book 8
Holding Out For Love, Coach's Boys Companion Story (*should be read between books 6 & 7*)
Cooking With the Coach's Boys
The Casteloria Royals Trilogy
A Prince on the Run, Book 1
The Physician to the King, Book 2
The Princess and the Bodyguard, Book 3
The Haunted Depot Series
The Secret, Book 1
The Depot, Book 2
A Merry Depot Christmas, Book 3
Men From the Double M Series
Josh, Book 1
Special Wishes Time Travel Romance
His Only Love
Her Long Road Home
Enza Series
Enza, Book 1
Other Fiction:
The Secret Admirer
Erin's Christmas Wish

A Fine Mess
The Ripple
Reluctant Guardian
Storytime Shorts, the First Collection

Stories by my Hemisphere cohorts:
Works by Billy Baltimore
Sasquatch: A Hemisphere Story (Emma Spaulding Paranormal Detective Book 1)
Djinn: A Hemisphere Story (Emma Spaulding Paranormal Detective Book 2)
Works by G Oldman
The Rise of the Watchman: A Hemisphere Story
Peril in the Park: A Hemisphere Story: Book 2
Works by Kit Nash
Some Assembly Required: A Hemisphere Story (RECTIFIER Book 1)